Bessie Ann was born into a farming family on
Dartmoor, so she enjoyed country life and animals.

BESSIE ANN

FREDDIE'S BIRTHDAY PARTY

AUSTIN MACAULEY PUBLISHERS™
LONDON * CAMBRIDGE * NEW YORK * SHARJAH

A CIP catalogue record for this title is available from the British Library.

ISBN 9781788788199 (Paperback)
ISBN 9781788788205 (E-Book)
www.austinmacauley.com

First Published (2019)
Austin Macauley Publishers Ltd
25 Canada Square
Canary Wharf
London
E14 5LQ

I would like to dedicate this book to my three grandchildren: Jack, Georgia and Heidi. Although past teenage years, this was written for them when they were small children.

A big thank you to my husband, Graham, who did most of the illustrations for me.

This is Rabbit Warren Hill
where the bunny family live.

RABBIT WARREN HILL

Jack came running out of his home and jumped on his bike – followed by his sister Georgia who climbed into the little carriage at the back that their grandad had made for her. "Goodbye," said Mrs Bunny as she waved to them.

They were going to Freddie's birthday party and met Heidi, who rode a red tricycle coming up the road to meet them.

Heidi lived in a little house called Leafy Thatch Cottage with her mummy, in the lane next to the field where Chippy the pony lived and she often gave him carrots over the fence as a special treat.

Chippy spent all day eating grass in the meadow, which he enjoyed very much, before going back to his stable in the corner of the field to sleep at bedtime.

The next friends they met were Sam and Sally Squirrel. Sam was the same age as Jack and they often took their little sisters for rides sitting on the back of their bikes.

Sam and Sally lived in the tree house, a very high walnut tree with a door at the bottom and lots of windows and another door high up which went out onto a balcony. They played all day with their brothers and sisters running around in the tree collecting nuts for their lunch.

Nearby lived Oscar Owl the postman. He would sit outside his home in High Rise Oak and watch them riding their cycles after he had finished delivering all the letters and parcels.

Their next stop was Prickly Cottage.

PRICKLY COTTAGE

This was where Chloe and Rebecca lived; they were twins and often wore dresses alike and rode on a bike for two called a tandem.

Then they all went to Mrs Willows pretty garden;
Torvill lived here under the shed and she often
left out lettuce for him to eat, but Torvill
had already gone.

Torvill had left home early. He rode a scooter and it was hard for him to keep up with his friends and he didn't want to be late and miss any of the fun at the birthday party.

Sometimes one of his friends would let him ride on their bicycle which he enjoyed very much. He was saving all his pocket money to buy one for himself to ride.

When they rode into the field Torvill was already there, so was Oscar and they both watched them arrive on their cycles.

Mrs Frog had made a lovely tea for them laid out on a big tablecloth, as they got nearer they could see all the lovely things to eat: lettuce sandwiches, carrot cake, hazelnut buns with a cherry on top, fruit flan, cheese on sticks, blackberry and lemon tarts, bottles of juice to drink and a big birthday cake with five candles on it for Freddie to blow out.

When they had all eaten their tea they all gave Freddie a birthday present: a kite from Oscar, a fishing net from Sam, a jar of jelly sweets from Sally, a sailing boat from Heidi. Torvill gave him a coloured ball, Jack – a colouring book, Georgia – some crayons, Rebecca and Chloe a scarf and socks.

"You still have a large present to open from your mummy," said Georgia.

"Please open it," said Heidi, "so we can all see what it is."

He took the paper off and it was a Penny Farthing bicycle.

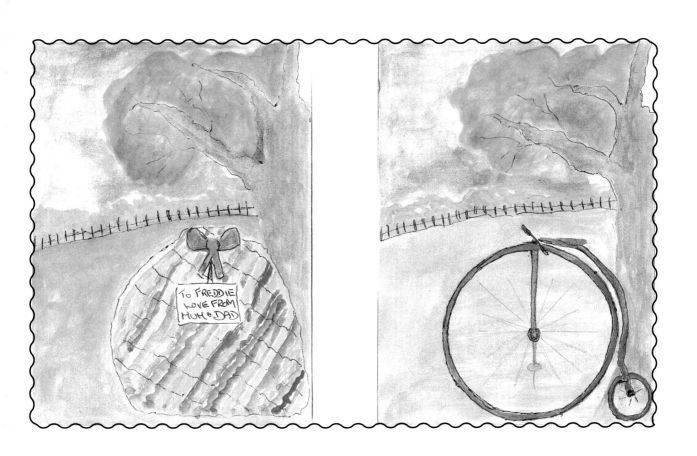

Freddie tried to ride it but he kept
tumbling and falling off.

"We will give you some help,"
said Rebecca as she ran forward.

Soon he was riding with no
help – and was very excited.

"Thank you Mrs Frog," said the friends, "we have had a lovely tea party and games to play. We all hope Freddie likes his presents and his new Penny Farthing, he can now join our bicycle club."
They all got on their bikes to ride home.

They all left to ride home led by Freddie on his
new Penny Farthing who was very safe riding on
it as he had a lot of practice all day long.
They were all eager to tell their mums and dads,
brothers and sisters what a lovely party they
had at Freddie's, as usual they were watched by
Oscar sitting up in the tree.

Can You Answer these Questions?

1. Where did the bunny family live?
2. Who made the little carriage that Georgia rode in?
3. What sort of cycle did Heidi ride?
4. Who did Heidi live with?
5. What was the pony called that lived in the field next to Heidi's home?
6. What was Sam's sister called?
7. What did they gather from the tree to eat?
8. What did Oscar deliver?
9. What were the twins called and what sort of cycle did they ride?
10. Who lived in Mrs Willows garden?
11. What was Torvill saving his pocket money for?
12. Whose birthday party did they all go to?
13. What did Freddie's mum and dad buy for him?
14. Who rushed forward to help when he kept falling off his new bicycle?
15. What did the friends say Freddie could join now he could ride his Penny Farthing?

1. Rabbit Warren Hill
2. Their grandad
3. A tricycle
4. Her mummy
5. Chippy
6. Sally
7. Nuts
8. Letters and parcels
9. Chloe and Rebecca – a tandem
10. Torvill
11. A bicycle
12. Freddie's
13. A Penny Farthing
14. Rebecca
15. Their bike club